D1415557

THE WORLD OF BEATRIX POTTER · PETER RABBIT ™

Peter Rabbit
and the Pumpkin Patch

FREDERICK WARNE

Published by the Penguin Group

Penguin Group (USA) Inc., 375 Hudson Street, New York, New York 10014, USA

Penguin Group (Canada), 90 Eglinton Avenue East, Suite 700, Toronto, Ontario
M4P 2Y3, Canada (a division of Pearson Penguin Canada Inc.)

Penguin Books Ltd, 80 Strand, London WC2R 0RL, England

Penguin Ireland, 25 St Stephen's Green, Dublin 2, Ireland (a division of Penguin Books Ltd)

Penguin Group (Australia), 707 Collins Street, Melbourne, Victoria 3008, Australia
(a division of Pearson Australia Group Pty Ltd)

Penguin Books India Pvt Ltd, 11 Community Centre, Panchsheel Park, New Delhi—110 017, India

Penguin Group (NZ), 67 Apollo Drive, Rosedale, Auckland 0632, New Zealand
(a division of Pearson New Zealand Ltd)

Penguin Books (South Africa), Rosebank Office Park, 181 Jan Smuts Avenue,
Parktown North 2193, South Africa

Penguin China, B7 Jiaming Center, 27 East Third Ring Road North,
Chaoyang District, Beijing 100020, China

Penguin Books Ltd, Registered Offices: 80 Strand, London WC2R 0RL, England

www.peterrabbit.com

The publisher does not have any control over and does not assume any
responsibility for author or third-party websites or their content.

Copyright © 2013 by Frederick Warne & Co.
Frederick Warne & Co. is the owner of all rights, copyrights and
trademarks in the Beatrix Potter character names and illustrations.

All rights reserved. No part of this book may be reproduced, scanned, or distributed
in any printed or electronic form without permission. Please do not participate in
or encourage piracy of copyrighted materials in violation of the author's rights.
Purchase only authorized editions.

With thanks to Ruth Palmer.
Manufactured in China.

Library of Congress Cataloging-in-Publication Data is available.

ISBN 978-0-7232-7124-6   10 9 8 7 6 5 4 3 2 1

ALWAYS LEARNING   PEARSON

Peter Rabbit
and the Pumpkin Patch

based on the original tale by

BEATRIX POTTER™

F. WARNE & C?

An Imprint of Penguin Group (USA) Inc.

After suffering through the stifling heat of summertime, the cool, crisp air of the autumn always makes one feel more lively.

It certainly had this effect upon Benjamin Bunny and his cousin Peter Rabbit!

Late one fall afternoon, Benjamin Bunny
set off with a hop, skip, and a jump into the
woods. He was going to see his cousins.

The woods were full of rabbit holes. And
in a sand-bank underneath the root of a very
big fir tree lived Peter Rabbit. Peter lived
with his mother and his sisters—Flopsy,
Mopsy, and Cottontail—in the woods behind
Mr. McGregor's garden.

Benjamin found Peter helping his mother wind
rabbit-wool yarn.

When old Mrs. Rabbit told Peter he could go,
Benjamin led Peter outside to the fir tree.

"Do you know what time of year this is?"
Benjamin asked his cousin. Peter gave a little nod.

"It must be harvest time in Mr. McGregor's
garden," said Peter.

"Yes," said little Benjamin. And then he whispered, "I'm certain that the parsnips are ready for Mrs. McGregor to bring inside."

"Pumpkin, too," added Peter; he did love pumpkin at this time of year.

It seemed such a shame to the little rabbits for the autumn harvest time to come and go, without a taste of beetroot, or a few nice ripe carrots for that matter; or even some late onions or sweet corn. They had missed the green beans altogether some weeks earlier; they had watched Mr. McGregor pull them off the vine and take them in to Mrs. McGregor, when all the bunnies had hoped for was several pods each!

After having supper with his relatives, Benjamin Bunny let his aunt think he had gone home. But later, when the moon rose over the woods full and clear, and Mrs. Rabbit had gone to borrow something from a neighbor, Peter sneaked out of the rabbit hole to the fir tree, where Benjamin was waiting.

The two were off to Mr. McGregor's garden. The moon led the way, and the little rabbits were in high spirits in that crisp night air. They felt that a great adventure was in store. But Peter couldn't help but wonder if they might be carried away by an owl. He suggested to his cousin that they not stay out long.

As they had done before, the little rabbits climbed down the pear tree into the garden, lit up by the moonlight. They saw some spinach leaves but kept going; they were looking for pumpkin and tasty parsnips.

But Peter heard noises, and began to go slower. Suddenly, he stopped.

Something frightening was looming near the pumpkin patch!

Peter grabbed Benjamin and ducked behind a wheelbarrow. When they were feeling braver, they peeked around.

"Why, it's only a scarecrow, wearing one of Mr. McGregor's old nightshirts," whispered Benjamin Bunny. He began to creep toward the pumpkins again.

Just then, the moon went behind a cloud, making everything go quite dark—Peter could barely see his cousin's white-tipped ears—and an awful screeching howl sounded nearby!

The bunnies were dreadfully frightened, and rushed nearly straight into a wall.

"Why, look, Peter!" said Benjamin Bunny after a moment, in his loudest whisper. "It's only Mr. McGregor's cat!"

Peter was trembling with fright. But when the cloud passed the moon, he could just see the cat inside Mr. McGregor's cottage. The cat was howling because she knew the bunnies were nearby.

Peter said he should like to go home anyway. He was worried that his mother would be back from the neighbor's and would be missing him by now.

But the two were nearly at the pumpkin patch, and Benjamin told Peter they certainly couldn't stop their adventure now. They found some parsnips on the way, which they began to nibble.

The bunnies had swallowed a few mouthfuls of the delightful parsnips when ...

Thump! Crash!

Poor Peter and Benjamin Bunny! They began to run, and dart, and zigzag away as fast as they could go, never once looking back until they reached the pear tree.

"There's nothing there," said Benjamin, surprised. The rabbits didn't know it was only a rake that had noisily blown over in the wind, and landed on a watering can.

But Peter was busy trying to scramble to the top of a compost heap, and safely back over the wall. Peter ran all the way home, and when Benjamin finally caught up to him at the sand-bank, they stopped to rest before going inside. They didn't want old Mrs. Rabbit to think they'd been in any trouble.

"I did so want a bit of pumpkin," said Peter wistfully.

As the two bunnies rounded the sand-bank, they saw a curious sight.

But this time, instead of running away in fear, the cousins hurried to get a closer look.

Old Mrs. Rabbit had carved a jack-o'-lantern for Flopsy, Mopsy, Cottontail, and Peter, and lit a candle inside it!

Oh joy! It was a party, with treats and lively games. But Peter seemed rather quiet. Mrs. Rabbit figured that he had got into some mischief and had learned his lesson about going out at night.

And Flopsy, Mopsy, and Cottontail and
Peter and Benjamin Bunny had creamy boiled
pumpkin—and pumpkin seeds for dessert.